I0539037

SHORTFALLS

A STAN WADE L.A. P.I. COLLECTION

THE STAN WADE SERIES

SHORTFALLS

A STAN WADE L.A. P.I. COLLECTION

JOHN HEGENBERGER

WILDSIDE PRESS

Copyright © 2018 by John Hegenberger.
All rights reserved.

Published by Wildside Press LLC.
wildsidepress.com

CONTENTS

INTRODUCTION

FICTION: DARK & LIGHT

These days, there's a heavy-weight emphasis on dark fiction. You can go to any number of "Noir at the Bar" events in major cities across the country.

It's as if the criminal element of popular fiction has won the battle against the dogged or clever detective and we all might as well lay down and die. It's grim, gritty, occasionally gory and heavy as sixteen tons. "Another day older and deeper in debt."

Maybe it started with Jim Thompson. Perhaps it's a mutation from Stephen King's popular horrors. Or we can blame James Ellory. Whatever the case, it doesn't matter.

Noir is only a sub-genre of mysteries, and not even that of fiction, itself. It's the single black crayon in a rainbow box of Crayolas. Thus, a good story, more often than noir, can and should be based on the more colorful aspects of reality. Optically, black is the absence of all other colors; the opposite of light.

And what's wrong with light? I like light. I like the Funhouse more than the Chamber of Horrors. I like Superman more than Batman. I like Arsene Lupin, Simon Templar, and Indiana Jones over Hannibal Lector or some soiled, addicted, vengeful ex-cop or ex-con. Let's have a little fun in this house. Open the windows, switch on the lights. "Come on baby, light my fire!"

This is not some crazy pipe dream. Stan Wade is a sort of realistic, self-deprecating and average guy who is inspired to figure things out and help other people. Sure, he gets in over his head and there are dark moments in his life, but he doggedly goes on (with a lot of help from his friends) and cleverly finds the truth, justice and the nostalgic, 1950s version of the American way.

In those days, which you still can watch play out on multiple TV channels, everybody worried about sputnik and the Bomb, smoked outstanding and mild cigarettes, loved Walt Disney, learned to surf and sing folk songs, watched color television and wide-screen westerns, drove finned gas-guzzlers while sneering at VW beetles, read trashy paperback books and gaudy ten-cent comics. Who does that today?

The stories in this volume are always bright, even if he isn't. They share a fondness for a time long gone too soon in a place that existed partly as a Hollywood fantasy and somewhat of a secret history of a hidden reality. Throughout it all, the tone is light, warm, yet much more jolting, bouncy and dangerous than cozy.

The events in Stan's stories are, in fact, light enough that we can confidently and comfortably believe they actually might have happened; certainly could have happened; definitely, absolutely, positively should have happened… give or take a lie or two. Just remember, Stan's #1 client is Uncle Walt, so his world and stories originate from "the happiest kingdom of them all."

So, take a moment now to relax, have fun, and return to those stirring days of yesteryear with Stan Wade, LA PI.

—John Hegenberger
The Heartland of Ohio
May, 2018

A WISP OF MEMORY

My head is killing me, for some reason. Probably the results of last night's poker game.

"I've been watching 'The Twilight Zone' on Channel 9." Norman sounds excited. "There's a new one, called the 'Darker Drink' on tomorrow night."

There's a sharp pounding in the back of my head and I can see the glowing veins pulse when I close my eyes.

Norm has a tendency to go on. He talks with his hands a lot. "It's the fifth show of the 1959 season. Something spooky and jokey for Halloween."

I'm feeling so miserable that I seriously consider falling off the wagon... again. Might even set fire to the damn thing. "So that's it?"

"I think good old Mr. Karloff's in it." He waves. "Stan, you look awful."

I wash down a couple of Darvons with what's left of a cup of black coffee and listen.

"Serling wants to meet you. Says he needs a good detective. Can you take the case?"

Sometimes an investigation goes nowhere and you're left wondering. This usually happens when Norman Weirick asks me for a favor. I'm hung up on another case at the moment; a big one, but Norm has always come through for me when I need his help, so....

* * * *

Fortified with medication, I wait on a cool stone bench in the Palisades Park where Montana meets Ocean Boulevard. There are tiny white sails on the water out beyond the Santa Monica Pier. Somewhere in that direction, an old neighbor of mine, Tod Browning, is sipping beer with his feet up. I'd have to remember to stop in and let him complain and reminisce.

It's windy. I sit and watch the sun struggle through the thick tapioca clouds as the TV writer approaches from the paved path.

"Thanks for meeting me, Mr. Wade." Serling winces slightly and stares out at the shrugging ocean below the bluff. Three fat ladies stroll by in short-shorts and floppy hats. One loses her orange skimmer in the breeze and has to waddle and ripple after it.

"My pleasure." I offer my hand. Serling shakes it, standing there. Then he lights a fresh cigarette from the stub of the one he'd been smoking. He looks out into a grey infinity beyond the bay. "I come here often to think and compose myself."

I wonder what that really means and pick an invisible piece of lint from my trouser knee. "How can I help you?"

"There was a guy I knew in the military back in 1947. Like me, he was wounded in Manila during the war and that gave us something in common."

The Pacific Coast Highway buzzes beneath the cliff's edge. Pain in my head hums along.

"Then he followed me into college on the G.I. Bill at Antioch, near Dayton, back in Ohio. We were casual buddies, but after graduation, I lost contact with him."

I watch a gull swoop in and perch on a nearby trashcan. It eyes me.

"I thought I saw him a couple of times in the last week. I want you to find him."

"I figured as much." The grey bird plucks at a catsup-covered French fry. "What's his name?"

"Sloan. Martin Sloan. He's about my height and build. In his mid-thirties with dark thinning hair. I heard once that he was a vice president at an ad agency, but I don't know which one."

"Where was it that you saw him?"

Serling doesn't sit down. Seems to want to dominate the conversation. "Last Sunday in Griffith Park, which was sort of funny. I was scouting a location for an episode of my TV series. You've heard of it?"

I nod and the pain flares behind my temples.

"He was near the merry-go-round there, but when I looked again, he was gone. Then, yesterday again on Lot 2 at MGM, where we're shooting an astronaut episode. We were struggling through a hospital scene and when I looked up again, he'd gone off."

The last time my body had felt like this was a couple of weeks ago in Frisco, when I'd been doped. Maybe I've been hit on the head too often. Supposedly, that'll kill you or leave you in a coma. "You say he was injured during WWII? I could do some checking for you with the local VA hospital. See if they have a line on his location. It might not pan out, however. Are you sure you want that?"

He takes a deep drag and rubs the back of his neck. "I guess, I could be mistaken. But I'd like to know for sure. Set my mind at ease." He flicks his cigarette away and the wind catches it, almost bringing it back to us. "It looked like him and I'd like to talk with him again, for old time's sake."

I rub the back of my neck, too. It feels good. Must remember to do it more often. I get up and step on the butt to make sure it's dead.

We settle up the financial arrangements of my employment and I listen to Anita Bryant sing "Till There Was You" on the radio while driving back to my office in the rear of the Brown Derby. The restaurant is now decorated with paper skeletons and fake spider webs for "Saturday's Spooky Selebration".

I put in a call to the VA and sit on hold for a long time with no luck. The admin department has no record of a Martin Sloan. It was a long shot.

I swallow a couple more Darvons. Too many of those little scarlet-and-grey capsules could kill me. I wonder about that.

On a hunch, I place a long-distance call to the Kettering Detective Agency back in Dayton, to see if they could get a line on Sloan. The girl Friday there takes down my information and says they'll get back to me with whatever they can dig up and a bill for services, of course. Of course.

Since it was still early Thursday afternoon, I figure I can drive over to Culver City and MGM Studios to find out if anyone else there may have seen this Sloan fellow during yesterday's filming.

I drop into the driver's seat of the tan Mercury where Hertz has put me in and steer southwest through a cross-hatching of residential streets. Stopped at a red light near a Lucky store, a man waves a Bible and shouts, "Repent, before it's too late." I look at my watch. 3:39. I drive on, passing the Motel Vacancy and feeling a little better.

Arriving at the fortress-like east gate of the studio on Culver Boulevard, I park on the street under an anvil sky and walk up to the guard house. The gate guard chews gum and knows who I am from past visits. After I pay him and explain why I'm there, he pretends to phone someone to get permission to allow me onto the lot.

I have to hoof it past the five-story-high Stage 6 with its huge sign on top still promoting the studio's latest blockbuster, BEN-HUR. I'm pretty sure this was the same building where Gene Kelly danced in "On the Town," "Singin' in the Rain" and "Les Girls." Even though I've been on the lot before, I still manage to get lost between all the narrow alleys and walkways. A pirate passes me in a golf cart and an Indian on a bike. Here in movie-land, every day is Halloween.

I see Fred Astaire in the distance, but don't say anything to him, since he's probably still mad at me for busting up his fight with a parking lot attendant at the Derby last week.

I get to Lot 2 and see from the clapperboard that Cayuga Productions is wrapping up a shot. Most the crew is skying out for dinner, but I corral a red-head who's still going over his lines. "You Rod Taylor?" Nobody except Gable and an old girlfriend of mine had a jaw like that.

He looks up annoyed and I know my ID has been positive.

Assuming an air of professionalism, I introduce myself with a business card. The actor seems annoyed, but curious. I like that and tell him why I'm here.

Taylor scrunches up his brow and thinks for a second. "Yeah, I saw the man you're talking about; he was standing over there next to the lighting truck. I thought it was Serling, himself, for a second. Then Rod… you know, the other Rod… came up from behind me, and when I looked back, but the guy was gone. Disappeared almost."

"That's it?"

"Hey, mate, I don't have a lot of time for questions. I've got to wrap this silly TV show and scoot over where they're making a real movie."

I've a habit of reading the industry trade journals. "What movie?"

He swells a little. "I'm starring in the <u>Time Machine</u> feature for George Pal."

Maybe it's the headache that makes me say: "The Puppetoon

guy?"

He gives me a look that would have made Jimmy Finlayson proud and deflates a little. "I don't need this. Besides, there's no audience for an anthology series on television these days. Especially one so weirdo, right? Probably get canceled in another week and forgotten a week later."

I shrug and let him get back to studying his script. Taylor will probably go far in his career. He might eventually get a job in a dog-food commercial.

I fish around in my pocket for a paper envelope and gulp down a few new Darvons dry. I can't find anyone else on the set knows who or what I was talking about, so I amble back to the gate and ask the guard if he remembers seeing Mr. Sloan. "As it happened, a man like that left here about this time yesterday as I was going off duty." Pushes his cap back with a thumb. "Went out the gate and headed north on Culver."

So, I go out the gate, passing Frank Lovejoy coming in with a stacked blonde, and head north on Culver, watching for a taxi stand or a bus stop, but founding neither. Pretty soon, up on one of the cross streets, I stop at the Jackson Market. A sandwich and a Pepsi sound good.

The little deli looks like a Jewish holiday. Rapahanna or something. A long meat case running along one wall, filled with stacks of cold-cuts and cheeses; dishes of cold-slaw, bowls of potato salad, jars of pickles and eggs. On the opposite wall, a short zinc bar stretches in front of a mirror cluttered with receipts signed by famous movie stars. Myrna Loy apparently had eaten here in the past, probably for free in exchange for the autograph.

Reflected in the mirror is the bar's lone patron, drinking a beer from a frosted mug. He takes a pull and sets it down on a paper napkin. I study him, because he fits Sloan's description and he looks almost exactly like my dead brother, Josh. Dark hair, lined brow, sharp eyes. Shorter than I remember, but I hadn't seen my brother in over fifteen years and he'd seemed a giant to me back then.

I stand there, gnawing at the skin on the inside of my mouth. The man turns from the bar, gets off his stool and limps casually away from me. He opens the door to the Men's room and goes in. My headache is gone and I never take my eyes off the Men's room door.

I shout an order for corn-beef on rye and soda, waiting for Sloan to return. He never does.

After a good ten minutes, I go into the Men's room, but there is no one there. And no back door. And no windows. Just a small humming fan in the ceiling to circulate the air. I look in the stalls and behind the door. I look for the Candid Camera guy, but can't find Funt, either.

"No exit," Serling says, when I report back to him that evening.

"I did find this." I hand him a wrinkled paper napkin. The word, "Carol" is written on it. "Mean anything?"

We're seated in my cramped office. Serling is imitating a chimney again and filling my discarded coffee cup with ashes. He studies the napkin and stares directly at me. At first, he seems stunned. Then he smiles.

"It's strange how one little thing can change everything else."

"Eh?" I was getting a new sinus headache from the writer's fumes.

"Sloan introduced me to my wife, Carol, back in '47. He was dating her at the time and I guess you could say that I stole her away from him."

"Do you think he's dangerous? Wants revenge. Maybe you should call the cops."

"No. Not after all this time. I've often thought about him. Feeling a little guilty, I guess. If it hadn't been for him, my life would have been a lot different. That's why I want to find him. To thank him."

The phone rings, interrupting Serling's soliloquy. My contact in Ohio tells us Martin Sloan had fallen out of a crab-apple tree ten years ago there and died of a concussion.

Serling's hand shakes as he applies his Ronson to a fresh Raleigh. "But, I saw him...."

"So did I." My chair creaks as I lean back. "Maybe it's a joke."

"I hope not."

That's interesting. I tell Serling that there must have been some sort of mix up and that I'd be happy to keep looking. His choice.

He shakes his head. "Thank you, Mr. Wade. I'm satisfied." Through a haze, he goes on: "I see things differently now. It's inspiring and nostalgic."

"So that's it? You hire me to find a guy who disappears and then turns out to have been dead for a decade. That's what I call fantastic."

"Or you could call it an errant wish; a wisp of memory. I've been reading a lot of Bradbury lately and looking behind me. It's time I looked ahead."

The literal and figurative smoke was beginning to signal a sneeze in me. Some of these creative types are a pain. I pinch the bridge of my nose and sigh. When I look up again, Serling has left my office, taking the napkin with him.

* * * *

The next night, Friday, on a whim, I think, I tune in "Twilight Zone" on CBS and watch Gig Young in something called, "Walking Distance". Based on what my pal Norman had told me, I'd expected the show to be spooky or jokey with Karloff in it. It is none of that. Maybe the network has switched episodes at the last minute.

But, when I ask Norm about it later, he doesn't seem to know what I'm talking about. He even claims not to recall that we'd discussed it the day before and even accuses me of trying to play trick-or-treat on him.

I decide not to argue the point, but to stop taking Darvons. I'd rather have the ache.

THE BAD SLEEP

A death in Hollywood can mean a lot, especially if the deceased is rich and famous. But the death of a wannabe, a nobody or a hopeful, even under extreme circumstances, can end up meaning almost nothing in this town.

"Okay. What's the gag?" The dark-haired guy almost knocks me over with the tang of his bourbon-laced sigh. "I get that you're a hot-shot L.A. PI, but I know damned-well that your name's not Sam Spade."

I sigh back, perhaps too heavily. "It's Wade." I nudge my slightly-worn business card lying between the salt and pepper shakers on the aquamarine table cloth. "Stan D. Wade."

People a lot smarter than James Garner have tried to read my kisser and gotten nowhere. Mine is an ordinary face, except for the streak of white hair that runs from my forehead to my crown. I stand five nine barefooted and do my best to give the impression that I can take care of myself in a fight. It's an expected part of the profession. No one wants to hire a PI who might easily get sand kicked in his face by Charlie Atlas. The truth unfortunately is that I'm allergic to the L.A. smog and almost got an eye punched out early last year.

I don't enjoy pain, but it seems to insist on following me around, so I tolerate it as a sort of cost of doing business.

Today's business has me and Garner squeezed together at a slightly-wobbly table in the back of Clifton's Pacific Seas Cafeteria. Outside on Olive Street, it's a chilly January afternoon in the low 60s. Inside, it's a Polynesian dreamland that had once impressed Jack Kerouac. I'm having the fruit nut torte. My perspective client eats the blue fin tuna with pineapple. Around us, the walls and ceiling are decoratively painted and festooned with a south sea décor capable of ruining even a shark's appetite.

"You know, this is the very place that inspired Walt to design Disneyland." I toy with my fork, separating a brown-sugared walnut from a hunk of baked fruit cocktail.

Garner doesn't look around, but breathes more bourbon in my direction. "Well, it'll be closing for good soon. It used to be my favorite hangout, but the joint has lost tons of money throughout 1959." He holds my business card up to the light. "Where's… the Farraday Building?"

"Nowhere, anymore." There's no point in telling him that it had burned to the ground over a year ago and that I haven't gotten around to printing new cards. "Did you want to hire me to investigate something for you or not?"

"I'm, uh, thinking about it."

"Well, think harder." I make a show of consulting at my dead brother's watch and then did a little name-dropping. "Marion Davies is going to be on *Hedda Hopper's Hollywood* tonight. I'm supposed to be her bodyguard at NBC."

Garner doesn't seem impressed. Just gives me a stare with his soft, brown eyes. "I'll bet you read the trades." The actor currently starring in Warner's *Maverick* series lets a scowl crowd his glamorous features which I consider are not unlike my own. "I'll probably regret this in the morning," and he again sighs booze at me, "but I'm running out of time and am sort of desperate. How do I know if you're any good?"

Despite his hesitation, I warm to him and decide to play the earnest-wiseguy card. "I'm like this city, hell, maybe even this restaurant. What you see is *not* what you get." That kind of statement usually sells them, or sends them packing.

Garner frowns. "Must be nice to work without a studio dictating your every move." He shrugs. "Okay, Mr. Wade. You're hired. I need a man to look into a murder that the studio says I committed. Jack Warner and his executive asshole, Steve Cromwell, are blackmailing me over it. Without cause, I may add."

"So you claim."

The actor grimaces. "A young screenwriter was found dead on the set at Corriganville. You know Corriganville?"

"Yeah, it's the outdoor standing set north of here." I fold my napkin and signal for the old guy who served our exotic meal.

"That's the place. Appeared as a backdrop for hundreds of Bwesterns and TV shows over the last couple of decades. The writer, with the unlikely name of Chris Chandler, was discovered shot in the head by persons unknown and the studio quickly hushed it up, threatening to pin it on me as a way to manipulate me to work additional hours and days beyond my contract."

"I'm supposed to snoop around and find enough evidence to clear you or save you from the studio's abuse?"

The stooped-shouldered waiter comes over with our check and we look at each other for a second. Garner hands over a Dinner's Club card and nudges my elbow. "You might even solve a murder while you're there."

He's having a little fun with me now, so I can't resist posing the key question. "Did you do it?"

"I figured you'd ask me that." He leans back, appearing quite at ease. "Of course I didn't do it." His dark eyes seem sincere. Unfortunately I can't go on location out starting tomorrow for a few days. I have something more important to do instead."

His mention of murder doesn't bother me; I have contacts in the police force that are routinely capable of handling that sort of crime. His mention of blackmail isn't worrisome, either; the studios have been paying that dirty trick for decades all over town. No, what bothers me is his "something more important to do instead."

"What's more important than showing up in front of the lights and cameras?"

He sips his bourbon and gives me a quick explanation, ending with: "Do you want the job, or not?"

I tell him how much I charge and wait to see if he'll change his mind.

The figure didn't faze him. He writes me a check right there at the wiggly table for the first week's retainer. "That's how long I'll be unavailable, so you're on your own, Mr. Wade."

I like being on my own with other people's money. It helps me sleep peacefully at night.

* * * *

Comes the dawn, and I take my sinuses and my T-bird for an airing past San Fernando west through Simi Valley, while listening to

Shimmy Shimmy Ko-ko-pop on the car radio. A catchy tune, indeed, but I turn down the volume when the car phone buzzes.

I speak into the jury-rigged device that my pal, Norman, has built into the Ford's dashboard. "To be honest, I don't know why I took the case," I lie to Suzi.

Her tiny voice comes back to me from the contraption's speaker. "We don't need the money, Standy. The agency is back in the black and doing well ever since that Jerry Lewis investigation."

"I know. I just don't like the way the major studios still think they can push talent around, that's all. Edd Byrnes and Clint Walker both bumped heads with Jack Warner last year. Now Garner says he's getting threatened by the same outfit. Plus... there's supposed to be a dead body involved."

"Standy, promise you'll be careful. I know you haven't been sleeping well lately, and I suspect that you're on one of your crusades again."

What a sweetheart! I bid her bye and turn the wheel, steering through Suzanna Pass. Marty Robbins is now crooning about *El Paso*. I wonder if I'll catch sight of one of those new Nike missile installations out here. They're designed to pop up from an underground bunker and roar into the sky, day or night, to take out enemy airplanes. Ever since the middle of the Cold War, whole families come out on the weekends and picnic in the area with peanut butter and jelly sandwiches, hot dogs and ants, hoping to see the silos open and the rockets elevate. *What a nightmarish image!*

I've been having a lot of sheet-clenching nightmares of my own the last few months. None of them had giant ants or rocket explosions, fortunately. Not long ago, I'd intentionally killed someone for the first time—a woman who was about to kill me—and ever since, I'd begun to suffer through troubled sleep. I guess it could be worse; I could be as dead as the guy in this case Garner wanted investigated. A little bad sleep is better than the big sleep any day.

Coming out of the Santa Suzanna Mountains, north of Los Angeles, I run into three miles of heavy construction along Highway 118. I get to spend a little time staring at stands of cottonwood trees along the roadside. A sodden, cloud-congested sky lends an uneasy dimness to the day. The wind rips wildly against the higher branches like a cataract pouring into a chasm.

Suzi may have been right about my being on a sort of crusade. Guilt has a way of making a fella do fascinating and foolish things.

Around forty-five minutes later, I arrive at the entrance to the western backlot and see that the place has been converted into a weekend tourist trap. Here families can "visit an authentic western town" and even witness an "authentic shootout." What Disney and Marineland have done for fantasy and ocean-view theme parks, Corriganville is trying to do for the cowboy experience, complete with "authentic horse shit."

The guard stationed at the entrance to the grounds wears his hat far back on his head and twirls a rope to get visitors into the western spirit. I show him a note that Garner had scribbled, and the friendly shitkicker lets me pass, casually spitting tobacco juice on my left front hubcap. I drive slowly, eventually finding the movie set portion of the ranch and park beside a row of dark blue electrical trucks that house the generators to power huge banks of lights and a couple of enormous wind machines.

The true reason I've taken the case is that it gives me a chance to spend time with celebrities; especially those from my youth. I've always have been a sucker for movie stars, ever since the days I'd sat in the balcony of the Jewel Theater and watched westerns and serial chapters flash across the big screen. Hell, I'd once worked as a stuntman at Republic Studios in order to appear in the background of low-budget oaters.

In these intense days of civil defense bomb shelters, Supreme Court racial rulings and alarming nightly news programs, everybody needs a distracting hobby. Other people collect autographs; I collect behind-the-scenes experiences and backstage relationships with film personalities. This Corriganville investigation gives me an excuse to again feel like I'm a part of those fun and foolish movies. *So sue me.*

And here, coming toward me, is a new old Hollywood star: Ray "Crash" Corrigan. He's wearing a long-sleeve tan and red cowboy shirt embroidered with white roses. His wide-brimmed hat has a scarlet cord around the crown. "You the dude that Garner sent?'

Growing up, I hadn't taken much notice of Ray Corrigan, since he wasn't as big a star as Roy Rogers or Hopalong Cassidy, but his face is familiar, since he played beside John Wayne in a handful of "Three Mesqueteers" features.

He'd put on about fifty more pounds since he'd played in his western movies, but the face was still familiar and he set a horse with ease. When he grinned and glad-handed you, you just had to smile back. At least, I did, anyway.

I'd heard that he'd invested well in the early 1950s by creating this little ranch and western village for use as a busy backdrop in the production of horse operas. Then, when television had blossomed, the place got even busier, until finally the aging cowpoke actor got the idea of opening it up so the public could walk the dusty streets of what felt like an old western town.

I show him the note from my actor/client and watch the big man carefully while he reads it. When he asks why Garner's not with me, I mention client confidentiality and smile convincingly, I hope.

Never one to turn down a role in a movie, Ray had kept his name in the credit crawl of several movies by continuing to play a second-string cowboy and even a costumed gorilla. Since then, he has used his notoriety to advantage with his self-names theme park.

Corrigan hands the note back to me, appearing perturbed and even a might guilty. He a jerks thumb down the main street to a small building behind the livery stable. "The body was found inside there... supposedly."

I step over the threshold of the equipment shed he's indicated and immediately feel the increased temperature within the enclosed space. Ray pauses in the doorway to slap dust off his boots. "Despite this being early January, the temperature in here is as hot as a July jalapeno."

I decide to verbally play along. "And as dry as an August arroyo."

He lets that one settle.

Standing inside this hot shack, sweat begins to form above my eyes; slowly they adjust to the darkness. I see a jumble of workman tools, camera and sound gear and a few broken props piled in the far corners of the single-room building. Tangles of cables, a stand of Klieg lights, a broken boom mic, a seven-inch reel tape recorder and an electrical switch box that likely was left over from *The Bride of Frankenstein*, and yes there's an irregular dark spot on the bare floor that has to be dried blood. Dread clings to me like cobwebs.

I swallow carefully and poke around a bit more. The metal power conduit box lays flat on its back trailing wires beside a stack of reflector panels and an old-time camera still locked into place on its tripod. Is that a tarnished timpani drum?

Still puzzled, I turn back to look at Ray's dark, hulking outline framed by the sunlight in the open door. "Any idea why the crime was committed here?"

"It's a secluded and controlled space." He scrapes the soul of his boot against the door frame. "The studio likes to have a controlling interest."

"What do you mean?"

He shrugs. "They want to stick it to the actors and writers. I'd side with Garner about fighting those corporate vultures, but I can't afford to lose this here ranch or the filming business it brings in. Best if I stay out of it."

The fond recollection of a childhood hero pops like a soap bubble. The image of Corrigan as a brave, courageous and bold cowboy takes a mental beating. Or maybe I'm just tired from lack of sleep. Either way, I figure Corrigan's not the killer, since his sympathy lies with the little man and his fears originate from the corporations that are getting larger every day.

Maybe it's the outfit I'm wearing that inspires me to give Ray a little advice: "My old pappy used to say, 'The bigger they are the smaller they're hard.' If we don't stand up against the big guys, who will?"

He grunts and gives me a hard stare. "Very clever, Mr. Maverick."

We stroll outside into the sunlight. Since the park was open to the public during the weekends, I know that Corrigan has at least one source of income that's not directly under the studios' control. I wonder just how profitable the place is. "Mind if I wander around a bit?"

He grins with ease and saunters off without another word.

I'm left feeling like my eleven-year-old self, back at the summer dude ranch where I'd watered, fed and curried my first horse. I'd been one with nature and the old west. That first ride out of the white slatted corral and along the dirt trail up the side of a shaded hill had made a new kid of me back then. *Like being baptized.*

You see a lot of western towns on television these days. All of them have rough-hewn hitching posts, leaking watering troughs, dusty boardwalks, and saloons with tinny pianos, general stores with cracker barrels, pickle jars and black pot-bellied stoves. Gazing around this mock cowboy setting, I recall that director John Ford once used Corriganville as the main set for his film, *Fort Apache.*

A buckboard rattles in my direction and something—maybe a hornet—causes the horse to rear up beside me, pushing the back of my calves over the upper edge of a watering trough. Instantly I'm plunged, soaked and startled, splashing and gripping rough wet wood, cursing like a three-legged bobcat. *Baptized, again.*

The driver, an old gal in calico, rides on oblivious, and leaves me to sputter and fend for myself. At the far side of the near-empty clapboard Cowtown, under the shade of a grove of oaks, I drip my way to a small circle of trailers and silver motorhomes. One of them has Garner's name taped beside the door. The key that he'd given me fits the lock and I clamber inside.

Still cursing quietly to myself, I change into one of his dry western outfits and look in the mirror. There's a handsome man in there, dressed as a gambling dude with string tie, ruffled shirt, trim vest and black hat cocked at the back of my head. I give the mirror a winsome smile. "Howdy, ma'am. My handle is Wade. Bret Wade."

The mirror is delighted to make my acquaintance.

What the hell; why not go whole hog? I find a gun belt and begin to buckle it on my hip when I realize my trousers have been designed for a ballet dancer. There's no zipper in the crotch. Now, of course, that very thought causes me to want to empty my bladder.

I have the tight pants down around my ankles and am seated on the trailer's throne, when I hear the front door pop open and muffled footsteps shuffle across the floor. I shimmy-shimmy back into my pants and come out of the cramped bathroom to see the tail end of some dude whisking back out the door.

A sheet of paper has been dropped onto the sofa and I pick it up. While unfolding the note, I catch a glimpse out the trailer window of the top of the redhead dude who'd delivered it.

The handwritten message reads: *Final warning. Get to work or go to jail for murder."*

I crumple the paper in my fist as I dash out the trailer door in pursuit of the messenger.

As soon as I catch up, I reach out and swing the guy around to face me. His eyes are tight and blue, his expression worried. But there is an ingratiating charm to his face, boyish, under a pile of sandy hair. He appears harmless, but I know that handsome looks can conceal a cruel temperament, especially in Hollywood.

I lean in on him to prove that even if I'm dressed silly, I mean business. "What's the idea?"

His eyes search for a way out of the confrontation. Then he eases back and gives me a half smile. "What do you mean?"

"Who are you?" I hold up the scribbled note so he'll have to stare at it. "What's the idea of this?" I thrust my right hand, clutching the paper, at his chest.

Somewhere behind us, a mule starts braying, and the redhead puts his hands up as if to push me away. His smile grows wider. Suspicion is no longer in his crinkled eyes. Just a nice guy out for a stroll. "Bobby Redford's the name." He sticks out his hand gladto-meetme. "What's this all about, officer?"

Yes, sir. A swell guy. And he thinks I'm a cop. Probably due to my gruff manner. I should use it more often. So I don't shake hands with him. Instead, I give him a stern look. "You an actor?"

He puts his hands down and leans back against a weathered hitching post. "I try to be. I'm in the episode of *Maverick* we're filming here. Guy gave me that message to put in Mr. Garner's trailer. Said it was important."

"What guy?"

He looks away, thinking. "The guy who works as an enforcer at Warners. He thinks he's a cop, too. So naturally, I...."

I know who he's talking about and quickly give him a description of Mr. Steve Cromwell, chief fixer for Jack's studio.

"Yeah, him. Why are you so steamed, officer? I've been hearing talk around about Chris Chandler getting shot."

"You know about that?"

The pretty boy puts his hands in his back pockets. "Yeah, I ran into him a couple of times in the equipment shed. I practice and playback my lines sometimes on an old tape recorder in there. He gave me a couple of pointers once from a screenwriter's perspective. Nice little guy. Sorry to hear about the shooting and all."

"Do you know who did it?"

Redford rubs the back of his neck. "Why would I know a thing like that?"

"Okay, then. Did Chandler ever seem nervous, or act funny?"

"All writers seem funny to me. Chris talked a lot about the pending Writer's Guild strike, if that matters. Guy wasn't sure if he'd walk the picket line or not."

If Redford said "guy" one more time, I'd belt him. "Did Chandler ever mention feeling threatened by anyone?"

"I really don't recall. I usually didn't pay much attention to his nutty ramblings. Sorry." I decide that Redford has a good shot at making it to the top of his profession, if he maintains that boyish grin. I doubt that he's a killer.

His eyes dart over my left shoulder. "Speak of the devil. There's the guy over there who had me deliver that note."

I turn to see Cromwell stepping slowly toward us. His wingtips are polished even out here in the middle of a fake one-horse town. His hands are raised, open-palmed, as if someone is holding a gun on him; one hand holds a burning cigarette. He seems calm and confident, like he thinks he owns the place.

Redford uses the opportunity to back away and I let him. Cromwell comes closer; collar is open, striped tie loose. His intense expression disappears momentarily behind a cloud of cigarette smoke. "You Wade?"

I nod.

"You're dressed awfully funny for a private investigator, fella." His voice is husky with a little catch in it. Probably due to too many coffin nails and all that East Coast money. "Yeah peeper, I know who you are and why you're here. Keep sticking your nose in and we'll sue it off."

"I've heard that one before and it doesn't faze me." I hold up the sheet of paper delivered by Redford. "Did you write this?"

He shakes his head, but I'm certain that he's lying. "Let me give you a little tip, Wade. Finding talent in Hollywood is not a problem.

Controlling it is the secret to success in this town."

"And you tried to control Chandler, but he wouldn't cooperate, right? Now you're trying to use his death to keep Garner in line."

The bureaucrat folds the paper, moving it to the inside pocket of his suit coat. "The studio doesn't give a rat's ass about some dime-a-dozen writer. Even a good one, like Browne, there." He points to a grey-haired guy in a baggy suit, standing under the awning of the Assay Office. "Like I said, keep out of this, fella, or you'll wind up in court." He walks away.

I let him go, because I'm more interested in talking with the writer he's pointed out. I'd met Howard Browne from a couple years earlier when he'd hired me to give him background and local color for a screenplay he was developing. In the Forties, he penned a series of "Halo" novels about a Chicago PI named Paul Pine. Good stories, and now I hear he's some sort of story editor at Warners. Garner was right; I read the trades.

As I approach, Browne glances my way over the tops of his bifocals. His face is round and his build is stocky, broad-shouldered. He has a script open in his hands. If anyone knows what happened to Chandler, it's bound to be a fellow writer, like Browne.

After I hail him and shake his moist hand, he wants to know why I'm dressed up like Maverick. I dodge the question and ask him about the young writer, Chandler.

"Yes, he seems a dedicated, hard-working cuss. A little moody, effeminate and a bit stand-offish, but probably Hollywood's next best hope, you know? I haven't seen him a couple of days."

"You haven't heard?"

"Heard what?"

"The word on the street is that your pansy writer's been murdered. Ask Corrigan. I think he found the body."

"What! That's terrible. I thought maybe he'd gone off to picket with the WGA, since he is, or was, a staunch union member. Damn! Now I'll have to get Wells Root to re-write the scenes we still need to shoot."

"Would the Writer's Guild be able to give me any background on him? Where he lives. Other people who knew him?"

"If you want to know stuff like that, you should ask Dobie. They often spent time together, I hear."

"Dobie? You mean Harry Carey, Junior?"

Browne gestures with his rolled script. "That's him over by the sheriff's office and town jail."

So it is.

* * * *

"Howdy."

Dobie Carey wears a western-cut sport coat with pads at the elbows and a maroon shirt with flowered tie. He's the son of actor Harry Carey. Both men have appeared in dozens of westerns, although seldom together. He's called Dobie because of his red hair, now thinning and faded to russet-blonde. His nickname is short for adobe, like the color of New Mexico clay at sunset, or at least that's what I'd read in the trades.

We stand on the boardwalk watching three cowpokes stroll past strumming guitars and torturing a squeeze box. The clouds behind them are silver. Spun glass rain is blowing in the west.

"I should have seen it coming." He wipes perspiration from his high forehead with the tip of his tie. "I'm here filming location scenes for a Jim Davis western, *Noose for a Gunman*. Chris and I ate lunch together over by the lake. But are you sure that she's dead?"

I stare at the Wanted posters on the wall outside the sheriff's office. One of the sketches looks alarmingly like Walt Disney. Distant lightning strikes and I taste the smell fresh-clipped grass, or maybe it's a reefer. "She?"

"Oh, that's a mistake." He breathes a sigh at me, just like Garner had. "Well, anyway…."

"She? Chandler's a woman?"

He shrugs. "Dressing like a man helped her get work from the studios execs. Adopted a masculine name like Leigh Brackett. Christine hated doing it, but called a 'necessary evil' in that deep Tallulah voice of hers."

I must be slipping. A good private investigator would have figured that out by now. I decide to blame the gaff on my lack of sleep. I tip my hat to Dobie like he's the best friend I have on earth.

He grins back. "Hope I helped. Gotta run. Davis needs me for a big gun-down scene."

* * * *

By day's end, I've confirmed that Corrigan was the person who had found the body and that he'd immediately informed Cromwell, who had taken it from there. The question is: taken it where? I go back to the equipment shed for a second look around. Among the saws, pipes, wires and camera parts, a small Movieola sits next to a brown bottle of Vitafilm, a liquid used to keep film fresh and limber as it passes through the editing device's gate. Nasty smelling stuff.

Dobie wasn't the only redhead in this affair. Redford had mentioned using the tape recorder. Maybe he wasn't the only one who'd recorded things on it. I switch on the machine and run the tape forward and back a few times over Redford's voice until the end. The tape runs out and I turn it over and re-thread it to play the other side. I hear a strong female voice say: "This is Christine Chandler speaking and I'm about to take my own life in protest. The studio slavery system must end. Let this act shine a light on the shadowy dealings of the crooks at the top of the system." I get that chill at the base of my skull, because I know what's coming. Still, I flinch at the loud report of gunfire.

"I'm sorry you had to hear that, Mr. Wade." Cromwell's voice behind me is harsh and sharp.

I face around and see he's holding a hatchet in his right hand. I try to mask my surprise with confrontation. "You knew all along about the suicide. Where's the body? And the gun?"

"All taken care of, fella." He moves in toward me.

"Sure. Except for this." I point to the recorder which has shut down now that the tape had ended. "You didn't know that she'd recorded a suicide note before shooting herself."

"She?"

"Fooled you too, eh? Even though you must have seen the body. Where'd you stash it?"

I take advantage of his confusion to throw a carpenter's hammer at his face.

He ducks and comes at me with the short ax raised.

I fight back with a screwdriver. It's the only sharp thing I can lay hands on.

The blade chops down, pinning the right sleeve of my western costume to the edge of a wooden table. Equipment parts and tools sail high, tumbling and clanging near my head. The bottle of Vitafilm strikes the planked floor and shatters into a rank, glittering puddle. The harsh stink envelopes us.

I cough, clutch the cool neck of the broken bottle and now have a sharp weapon in each hand.

But the blade of the hatchet is wrenched free from the table just as I get to my feet. I bite my lower lip. The bitter blood and tawny odor makes me woozy, but I dodge left, past a broken tripod to thrust my hip into the side of the table sending it and the tape recorder skidding into Cromwell. The hatchet is heavy enough to take him off balance. I stumble through the fumes, swishing the screwdriver at his head. I catch a knee in my chest for my trouble and slam back on my ass. The cost of doing business.

He laughs. "Everything's been taken care of… except you and that tape."

The door opens behind us and I see a gorilla lumber in and grasp Cromwell by the shoulders. The ape raises up the man and tosses him into a stack of film cans, which skid and clatter, almost drowning out the loud crack of Cromwell's head hitting the iron base of the overturned Klieg light.

I watch dully as the gorilla's head slides back to expose the sweat-drenched face of Ray Corrigan. Then a dark red liquid seems to ooze down over the lens of my camera eye and it's fade to black.

* * * *

I come out of a bad sleep with a raging headache, into the fresh air.

"I'm never wearing that thing again," Ray says with satisfaction. "And I'm never buckling under studio pressure again either. I'll tell the world." He had finished with a screen test for a new version of "The Lost World" at 20th Century Fox when he'd interrupted my dance with Cromwell and had him escorted off the site. I realize that the studio fixer probably won't ever be charged with abducting Chandler's body or even blackmailing Garner, but I promise to myself that I'll get him on an assault charge.

While Corrigan climbs out of his monkey suit, I thank him again for saving my butt. We're seated in his office at the back of the saloon. "I felt bad when I learned that Cromwell had taken the body away, but I didn't want any more trouble." He shrugs into a new western outfit; this one has includes a grey shirt with snap-button pockets big enough to hold paperback novels. "So now are you going to tell me why Garner didn't show up for shooting here? Browne was complaining earlier that he had to re-write the 'Iron Hand' script to replace your client with Jack Kelly."

The elder cowpoke and I ambled together past a stage coach drawn-up in front of the Silver Dollar saloon. I've changed back into my dry clothes, intending to leave the Wild West behind, but I guess Corrigan has earned an answer to his question about the actor's absence. "It's no big secret." I watch a dust-covered hombre wrangle a group of tumbleweeds down the street. "Garner's tied up for a week in a hospital."

"Sick?"

"They're testing his blood. He told me he has a rare type and his agent's son will die without it."

"And you believe him?"

"Yes. I do. So, they need him to rest and eat and then they draw a pint or two every few days."

"Ugh! But yeah, that sounds like Jim, after all. I hear he'll go out on strike against the studio, if SAG follows the WGA's lead. Maybe I will too. I guess it's good to stand your ground on principle."

"Helps you sleep at night, too."

The mayor of Corriganville waves to me from in front to the fake Chinese laundry.

I wave back and drive off into the lemon sunset, listening to 'Running Bear' on the car radio.

* * * *

The Ventura County cops never did find the gun or Christine Chandler's body. She lies asleep, I guess, buried somewhere in the hills under western skies. Or maybe she's weighted down in Corriganville's man-made lake where they shot the underwater scenes of the Black Lagoon creature back in 1954. In a way it doesn't matter, since she had no family than anyone knew of. *Just a nobody.*

At the back of my mind, I can't shake the feeling that I've simply been a catalyst for events again; that my nosing around has caused other individuals to act against their better nature. Ask enough questions and things happen. Kick enough sleeping dogs and someone gets bit. One more wicked image to trouble my sleep.

Like I say, I don't enjoy pain. It's just part of the cost of doing business. And I swear to God, my business with Mr. Steve Cromwell is far from over, fella.

THE MAGNIFICENT SCORE

The doorbell rang.

Which is weird, because my tiny office at the back of the Brown Derby restaurant has no doorbell. Neither does my forty-eight foot boat moored at its slip in Santa Monica, for that matter.

"Ding. Dong. It's not Avon."

No, it was Norman Weirick fooling around again. I should have known. He'd been acting funny throughout all of 1959, since I'd taken him on as an "assistant" private investigator, and now in the early days of 1960, it looked like I was in for another year of his clever yet unpredictable shenanigans.

I shuffled a few papers around on my battered desk in order to appear busy. "Hey, buddy. What's doing?"

Norm dropped into the creaking client chair and adjusted the Coke-bottle lenses on the bridge of his nose. "MGM is trying to put United Artists out of business."

I couldn't help tightening my brow. It's something I often did when Norm obliquely started a conversation. Pretty soon after that, I usually got a headache. "The big studios are still reeling from the WGA strike. And they're always battling each other behind the scenes. Som what's the big deal?"

He rolled the swivel chair forward two inches, right up to the front edge of my desk. "The big deal?" His voice was akin to that of a young screech owl. "The big deal is…."

The phone bell rang.

I raised a palm. "Hold that thought." Picking up the receiver, I gave out with my usual opening line. "Stan Wade, detective. How can I help?"

There was a muffled sound on the other end of the call. Then: "Uhm, is your refrigerator running?"

I hung up and looked eye-to-eye at Norm. "Go on."

Outside my office door, some poor soul dropped a tray of glassware. Slivers tinkled down the tile hallway, sliding out toward where the restaurant patrons ate lunch. *Just another typical day at the office.*

I returned my attention to Norman, who told me about director John Sturges, whom I'd heard of due to the success of *The Old Man and the Sea.* He went on to reference film composer Miklos Rozsa, whom I'd *never* heard of, but should have due to the grandeur of his film score for *Ben-Hur.* I knew a lot about movies. Nonetheless, what I know about movie *music*, you can put in a piccolo.

My eyes were about to glaze, and then Norm mentioned that Steve Cromwell was leaning on Sturges. I'd had recent dealings with Cromwell while on a case up in Corriganville. Jack Warner's chief fixer had an underhanded technique of blackmailing the studio's actors to keep them under control. I'd tried to get evidence to disrupt this ploy, but he was mobbed up tight. I itched to go another round against him and this Sturges/Rozsa thing sounded like a perfect opportunity.

"So Sturges is making *The Magnificent Seven* at United Artists." Norm laced his fingers together on top of his burr haircut. "And he wants Rozsa to do the score." His elbows extended out to each side like a human TV antenna. "But Rozsa's under contract with MGM for the remake of *King of Kings.* He's stalled out inspirationwise and wants to moonlight with Sturges."

"Okay. I follow so far. What's this have to do with Cromwell?"

"MGM, by the way, would love to see UA fail, so they can buy them out."

"I'm not interested in corporate takeovers." I leaned back, accidently banging the top of my chair against the wall. My face must have given away my impatience. I hoped so.

"But imagine…." Norm lowered his arms and spread his hands wide over my desk, almost knocking over a stack of unpaid bills. "If one studio acquired or crippled all the others, they'd hold a monopoly over the industry. It'd be a nightmare."

"Where does Cromwell come into it?"

He swallowed, composing his thoughts for my benefit. "MGM doesn't want to spook Rozsa, so they've hired Cromwell to strongly convince Sturges to get someone else to write the film score. You follow?"

I straightened the pile of past due notices. "Force him how?"

"Ah, now here's the interesting part. Remember that red-headed lady found strangled and dumped in the bushes near the Arroyo High School a couple of years back?"

"No. And how do you know about all this?"

"Research. For my new novel. It's gonna be a western with werewolves."

I almost put a hand to my face. "What's your point, Norm?"

"My point is: Cromwell is threatening to tell the cops that he has evidence that Sturges was the killer."

"Does he?"

"I don't know." He slumped a fraction of an inch. "Sturges just wants Cromwell off his back so he can concentrate on his new movie. When I heard about it all, I immediately thought that you might... want to... look into it?"

"Indeed." It sounded like Steve Cromwell was up to his usual dirty tricks and that made me smile. "Yeah, I think I might." *But first I need a little research of my own.*

* * * *

I began by asking Suzi to look into Norm's story. I wanted to know more about Rozsa and Sturges. And what really interested me was the murder of the red-headed woman.

Suzi, my fiancée, ran her own investigations agency. We were partners in most senses of the word and planned to officially tie the knot in a few months. She had a couple of cracker-jack operatives who could track down info on Rozsa and Sturges, and I knew she would take a personal interest because of the murdered woman.

Usually all this would cost me an expensive dinner and floor-show, maybe at Earl Carroll's club, if it was still open. Under those conditions, Suzi would get me the facts, ma'am, *pro bono* on this case, or *moi bono*, if I knew Suzi. And I did.

Norman arranged a three o'clock meeting for me with John Sturges at the UA lot. As the director of *Last Train from Gun Hill* took my hand in greeting, I gave him my card and noticed that he never stopped moving. Tapping a pencil on the desktop. Shuffling through papers and glossy photos. An all-action sort of guy.

I took a seat on a couch half-covered with scripts and storyboard drawings, hoping it would settle him down. "I hear Cromwell is pressuring you to get a new composer."

He paced four steps back and forth in front of a shaded window that faced a duck pond. "Can you get him off my back?"

"I can try. If we work together on it."

His dark eyes darted out the window, as if searching for an image that might be used in a photo shoot. There was a muscular sense to his face that made him seem constantly serious.

"I'll take any help I can get against the leech. What'll it cost me?"

I smiled. *This is your lucky day.* "No charge. It's personal."

That stopped him in his tracks, running his fingers over the top of his head, as if to slick back the hair that wasn't there. "I don't want any trouble. I just want to make movies unencumbered, understand?"

I nodded agreement.

His voice was raspy, perhaps from barking too may orders on the film set. "MGM's *Ben-Hur* sucked all the ticket sales and profit out of the Christmas trade and left my *Never So Few* playing to empty houses." He started bouncing a baseball off the office wall. A real bundle of nerves.

"Yeah, I get it. From what I've heard, MGM wants to put UA out of business. So, why don't you relax and tell me the details about Cromwell?"

We talked for another ten minutes, and I honestly didn't learn anything that Norm and Suzi hadn't already told me. At least, with this preliminary visit, I'd made a positive impression on Sturges. It was time to move on to the main attraction, a face-to-face interview with Cromwell.

* * * *

Late that afternoon, during the drive over to MGM on Washington Boulevard, I listened to the news on the car radio. On this cold, clear Groundhog's Day of 1960, Senator Hubert Humphrey came out of his hole to say that the young, Catholic candidate for President, Jack Kennedy, was too young and too Catholic. I recalled that Suzi currently had an open case working for Kennedy's campaign. She'd told me last week while we were playing tennis that she'd uncovered some mighty interesting dope on Richard Nixon. However, that was her investigation; mine was here at MGM.

I met Norman at the august, ancient studio still in operation, despite the unions and independent film makers. The backlot had seen better times in earlier years while filming classics like *Gone With The Wind, Gaslight*, and *Singin' in the Rain*. Recently, it had appeared in a couple of TV episodes of "The Untouchables," clearly on its way downhill.

A surprisingly strong wind blew the heat around us. I remembered taking a tour here once as a ten year old. My fifth-grade class had walked among this mysterious, colorful blend of exotic locations, surrounded by costumed performers and massive camera equipment. At the time, I'd wanted to run away and hide, so I could live here forever. Now, the building facades crowded in on each other, drab, plain and dull.

I said something about it to Norm. He shuffled along behind me, hands in his pants pockets. "Location shooting is the new rage in Hollywood. Camera equipment these days is a lot more portable and easy to handle."

Something not so easy to handle was our meeting with Steve Cromwell. I was familiar with his kind of corporate underhandedness. He specialized in intimidation and extortion. For years, the Mob had wanted to get into the movie industry and currently the Fixer was a far as their influence extended... or so I believed.

I glanced at my watch. Quarter to four. *How had it gotten to be so late?*

A woman with cat-eye glasses ushered Norm and I into Cromwell's office. The room was cast in antique Spanish with nail-studded chairs, leather cushions and a gray-green olivewood desk.

The Fixer dressed like a corporate executive; what is commonly called an "Organization Man." Here in sunny Hollywood, he'd be much too warm in a gray flannel suit, so he wore a shiny blue three-piece of what's known as sharkskin.

Cromwell's teeth gleamed whiter than normal, as if they'd been re-touched by the makeup department. His black hair set plastered close to his head without any parting. His eyes were as cold as two dimes frozen in ice. In fact, they reminded me of those plastic novelty ice cubes with dead flies in the center.

We didn't shake hands.

I told him why we were here and what we knew. He didn't care. He set fire to a cigarette with a Zippo from his vest pocket and puffed smoke in my general direction, squinting. I knew he commonly twisted the truth and bullied people without remorse. He was a Mob bureaucrat who could extinguish my little private eye agency with a couple of phone calls… yet I didn't care.

Norm tried to act tough. "I've heard you're threatening John Sturges."

Cromwell blinked at him and flicked an ash. "Don't you have to be at work somewhere?"

My pal seemed stuck for a comeback, so I leaned forward. "Disney gave him the day off."

Somehow that gave Norm a shot of babbling courage. "Yeah, and you accused the director of murdering some… some red-headed hooker last seen alive after midnight back in June of '58."

The Org Man looked at me and took a deep drag. "No idea what you two are talking about, Wade." He exhaled. "But you better knock it off."

It was a flimsy, magnificent challenge on Norm's part. Bluff the bluffer. Unfortunately, we all knew that the L.A. County Sheriff's department had no active suspect, so if Cromwell fingered Sturges, the cops would quickly land on the director.

Norman went on now to pretend that the Sturges had been with him the night of the murder, working on a new piece of camera equipment. "It'll pan automatically during a wide shot from a moving vehicle."

I could see that Cromwell still wasn't buying it. He stared at us rigidly. *What does he know that we don't?*

His face became darker. He was about to speak, when, without knocking, the middle-aged woman with cat glasses came into the office. "JR wants you." She acted as if Norm and I weren't there.

Cromwell got up and straightened his vest, keeping his eyes on us. "You should be leaving, fellas." He moved around the side of the desk, heading for the door and leaving his cigarette burning in an ashtray.

I got up, too. "Yeah." I reached over and crushed out his butt. *Tough guy to tough guy.* "We've got a crime scene to visit."

* * * *

From reports in the newspapers from June 23, 1958, we could see photos of the woman's son, Jimmy, and the location where the body had been found by a guy walking his dog late at night. Jimmy looked disconnected from events, too young to fully comprehend what had happened to his mother. According to the newspapers, she'd last been seen alive at the Desert Inn in El Monte.

There was no sign of her here now, a year and a half later. A clump of bushes had grown into the thicket where her body had lain. The gravel path next to the fence containing the athletic field still seemed to carry the trampled imprints from a troop of flat feet. Searching the area where the dead woman had been discovered only gave Norm and me a wrapper from a 5th Avenue candy bar and an empty RC Cola bottle.

My friend hung onto the bottle. "Two cents deposit."

I scanned the empty baseball field, watching a breeze push a stand of short pine trees back and forth. I was tempted to wave back. The twilight clouds raced along a darkening horizon. "Looks like it's fixin' to rain." Within the shadows below the trees, I thought for a moment I saw a deer with frightened eyes, but it bounded away. *Probably just a dog.*

Off in the distant row of cheap houses that backed up to the school lot, someone hammered. It was a little late in the day for putting up aluminum siding, but I could see two men in overalls climbing down a scaffolding to pack up their tools.

A piece of grit blew into my left eye. I rubbed it and let it water, enduring blurred vision for a couple of seconds. Thinking of the woman who'd been dumped at this innocent site, I wondered if all of reality was simply a blurred vision, like a ghostly half-moon drifting among clouds, a big nowhere.

Norm nudged me awake. "You wanna getoddahere?"

I took a breath and let it escape. "Yep."

* * * *

In my line of work, sometimes you have to just push stuff together or noodle around, before something important happens. Thus, late next morning, Norman and I drove across town to El Monte. Bobby Darin sang "Mack the Knife" on the car radio to which Norm snapped his fingers. I'd grown sick of hearing the song weeks ago, so I switched stations to catch the news. Some Negro students were staging a sit-in at a Woolworth's drug store in North Carolina. Hoagy Carmichael was scheduled to appear on tonight's episode of "Laramie" and Andy Griffith would be a guest on "The Garry Moore Show." The USA had sent up a weather satellite that Norm swore was actually designed to spy on the Russians.

I found the Desert Inn on the south side of the street and parked my Thunderbird in the lot next to the entrance. Norm and I stepped inside to find the place almost empty. Beyond the restaurant's wide windows, the traffic on East Valley Boulevard hummed both ways. *Clearly a breakfast spot in the mornings and a watering hole at night.*

The long bar in the back of the low-roofed building gleamed from polished brass and backlit bottles. Leather chaps were nailed to the wall over the fireplace housing white birch fake gas-fired logs. Twin chandeliers fashioned from old wagon wheels hung horizontally over the plush booths. Little cowboy hats and boots decorated the napkins.

"I'll be darn. I think I just remembered this joint." Norm slid into the end booth and held up his hands as if he were taking pictures with an invisible camera. "This is where I snapped shots of Brando meeting a guy to pay off the Santa Anita bet."

A middle-aged, middle-weight cowgirl wearing a cap gun in a plastic holster ambled over to take out order. Her Desert Inn name tag said, "Large Marg." The laminated menu didn't offer much more than steak and eggs, Texas style, whatever that was.

Norm rubbed his palms together in anticipation. "I'm thirsty. Bourbon and branch water."

She popped her gum. "Oh, getting in the mood of things, huh?"

My friend grinned and pushed his glasses up his nose. "I'll take that as a compliment."

I wasn't sure where their conversation was going and didn't try to sort it out. Norm is often weird, like I said, and causes me to get a headache. "Coffee and OJ. No, make that a club soda and lime, please."

She scribbled on her order pad. "You a friend of Bill W?"

"No. Just him." I jerked a thumb at Norm. "And like him, I'm thirsty."

She scowled and popped gum again. "Coming right up."

I caught a strong whiff of Tabasco sauce blended with cigar smoke from two booths over, where a couple of beefy geezers scarfed down ham and eggs. No one was at the bar, this time of day.

"Right there." Norm gestured over by the phone booth. "Brando was standing right there and he had no idea I was taking pictures with my Minox spy camera. I got lots of shots of him paying off the…" His voice drifted away.

I looked up at him and saw that his mind was a million miles away.

He screwed up one side of his face in an evil grin. "I think I just solved the case."

* * * *

"You kept the negatives?"

We stood in the semi-dark of Norm's cluttered rental home near the new Dodger Stadium.

"Look around. I keep everything." Norm sloshed the fluids in a metal pan under the red light that hung above the sink. "Some of my old comic books will be worth a fortune before you know it."

I leaned over his shoulder to study the image developing on the 8 x 10 and caught a lung full of rank chemical fumes. "How'd you get these's photos without anyone noticing?" I stifled a cough.

"The mini-camera was inserted in the spine of my hardback edition of *Tarzan and the Ant Men*."

Of course, it was.

He held a dripping photo up with a pair of metal tongs. "Look. See that couple standing at the bar behind Brando? That guy next to the hot chick is Cromwell, right?"

A smudged and blurred man had an arm around the same woman I'd seen in the newspaper photos. She'd been seen with a man at the Desert Inn hours before her body was found in the field beside the high school. The cops never knew what the guy looked like for sure. Squinting now at Norman's photo, neither did I. "This is a mess, Norm. We can't make positive ID of Cromwell based on this fuzzy image."

"No. But the wickedly cool thing is, he doesn't know that." He waggled his eyebrows like Groucho. "Lemme see what I can do to fix the photo, so you can bluff him. I saw them do that trick on '77 Sunset Strip' once, and the guy confessed all over himself."

Yep, Norm is a little weird at times, but he'd saved my life last year during a case involving Ian Fleming. And I desperately wanted to get the goods on Cromwell. So much so, that it almost made my mouth water, as much as my eyes were from the pan full of chemicals. So, yeah, maybe a bluff *was* worth a try. "Where's your phone?"

"Over there, next to the ham radio."

For a scientific guy, Norm surprised me by having an old candlestick telephone, made of brass with a dial on it. I hefted it the way Bogart would have and called Cromwell's number at MGM. When he came on the line, I again tried to convince him that Sturges had an iron-clad alibi. I couldn't understand why the Fixer was trying to incriminate the director, instead of the composer.

"Simple, Wade." The enforcer's voice came back. "The studio doesn't want to come down hard on the orchestra guy. They need him to cooperate and perform at his best, so they sent me to stop Sturges from using him after hours on the side. You understand."

I didn't like being lectured to. "I've got news for you, Cromwell. You were seen at the Desert Inn with the redhead. We happen to have photographic proof from that night. We can pin the murder on you, or you can back off Sturges. Your call."

I was attempting to blackmail a blackmailer. In a way, it made us somewhat alike. *Forget that!*

The line went quiet for a heartbeat. "I've got to be at the Hollywood Bowl in three hours, fella, to check out security in the area." He sounded bored, and yet I caught an edge in his voice. "Meet me there with your so-called evidence and we'll talk."

I hung the receiver back on the hook and looked at it as though the Fixer's voice lived inside it. Then, I got to work.

* * * *

Despite frequent indications to the contrary, I'm a not stupid. And up to now, Norm probably could have handled the entire case all by himself, but the circumstances were turning dangerous, which meant it was time for me to take full control. I also took a couple of precautions before heading out for the Bowl.

Last October, I'd attended a Moonlight Jazz concert here at the amphitheater. Thelonious Monk and Sarah Vaughan had played long into the night under the stars, accompanied by Count Basie's orchestra. I wondered what Rozsa thought of hot jazz.

As I drove up Highland Avenue north of Hollywood Boulevard, I passed a backhoe digging a trench along the side of the road to help drain off water from the recently installed fountains in front of the concert shell.

Cromwell and I met in one of the picnic grounds beneath the low-hanging palm trees. The pale blue shell of the amphitheater looked like the entrance to a man-made cave set near the side of the Hollywood Hills.

I didn't plan on getting into a fight with him. I found Cromwell leaning elegantly against the side of his Caddy, putting the flame of his Zippo to another cigarette.

I gave him my story and a look at the photos that Norman had hastily re-touched. From the flash in his eyes, I knew I'd hit pay dirt. *So he was there. And he's buying it.* I showed him the negatives as proof of good faith.

He inhaled deeply, tossed away the cigarette and reached for the film.

The flames from his discarded fag crackled in the dry brush beside us. Cromwell didn't seem to care. It had been a hot spring and a hotter summer, scorching the foliage and baking the earth throughout the area around the Hollywood Bowl.

I backed up not having planned on a forest fire. If we didn't stop it quickly, the whole hillside soon would be burning. A stiff wind now could feed a wild fire, baking, burning and destroying everything for acres in every direction.

When I looked back at Cromwell, he had a black gun on me. "Give."

The flames crawled across the trail behind him.

I stood there with my hands raised, just like in some cheap cowboy or gangster picture. A gangster picture where I'd be the victim. "Firestorm at the Hollywood Bowl.

"You know...." I stretched my neck to keep an eye on the fire growing behind him. "We're both in big trouble here."

He ignored the sounds of the flames. It dawned on me that maybe he'd planned the fire all along. *It'll cover my burnt remains after he shoots me.*

I had to stall him off, or distract him somehow. I tried another bluff. "Like you, I've been around the track a few times and have contacts in the cops and FBI. Each of them is holding a sealed envelope with copies of these photos, so you'd be wise to plan a long trip out of the country."

The .38 in his fist drifted slightly to the left as he sighed. "Bull shit."

A burning branch tumbled down a slope setting fire to a patch of brambles. A brown rabbit leapt and scampered away.

He came forward and felt in my coat pockets, under my arms. Circling around, he patted my hips and waistband.

The heat became intense. The flames licked along the edge of the path where we stood and rippled up a vine-wrapped tree trunk.

I scanned the area, but saw no one coming or going. "So, I guess we should head out, eh?"

"Down on your knees."

I didn't move, knowing that if I did, I wouldn't ever be getting back up again.

He slammed the left side of my head with the flat of his automatic and I slumped.

He came closer. "I'm going to enjoy this."

Fire danced high behind him. Dark smoke rolled over my face. He reached out and caught me by the necktie. My right hand dangled loosely beside my left foot. The Ruger .22 came out of my trousers from my left ankle.

His eyes widened. *He's going to shoot.*

A huge plume of hissing gas blew up from a fallen log. The flare caught his attention enough that I swung my left fist up under his chin. He went down like a bag of beach sand. I grabbed for his gun. It went off next to my right cheek. Lancing pain pierced my ear. I couldn't hear a thing. I waved my pistol around wildly, unable to find him in the vortex of flame and swirling darkness. Burning leaves drifted down into my face and hair.

Suzi had been my backup, watching through binoculars from further up the hill. It never occurred to either of us that Cromwell would be stupid enough to start a fire. By the time she got to me, my ears were ringing and my face felt like a mask of peeled flesh.

In the glut of roiling soot and heat, we couldn't find Cromwell's Caddy, but I caught sight of a string of silent fire trucks rounding the curve in the parking lot. Suzi got me into the back seat of my T-bird and sped us down the hill through clouds of dense smoke.

* * * *

I learned a major lesson that day: never back a rat into a corner. You just might find that you're the one who is trapped.

When we got to Hollywood and Vine and rode the elevator up to Suzi's offices in the Taft Building, she washed the blood from my ear, kissed me firmly and forced me to go to a local clinic for vision and hearing tests. The doctor there patched the side of my head and wrote out the word, "tinnitus" on a prescription pad. I told Suzi I felt fine and she punched me in the stomach, knocking my breath out.

Hours later, we learned that the fire had been quickly contained. Someone had used a nearby backhoe to re-direct the flow of the fountain water from in front of the stage to help extinguish the flames.

Suzi inspected my bandaged head and spoke directly into my face, slowly. "You could have died in all that chaos, Standy."

I struggled to read her lips. "I love it when you call me that pet name."

She smiled and sighed.

"Cromwell let me live. I'm sure that means he bought my story about copies of the photos being held by the FBI. I've got an edge on him now and I'm going to find the best way to put him out of business."

Suzi called Sturges to relay the news that the Fixer probably no longer posed a serious threat. Next, I wanted to let Rozsa know that he could go ahead with the score for *The Magnificent Seven* movie. She liked the idea of meeting the music man in person, so I got high-jacked to his suite at the Bel-Air. *What the hell. Why not?*

Rozsa had a beautiful set of rooms in the hotel up Stone Canyon Road. MGM always goes first class. The suite was decorated in gar-den colors, and sunlight streamed in through shear curtains. Through an open window came a cool breeze and the laughing sounds from a swimming pool two stories below.

When I entered, Rozsa was absorbed in playing something on the piano. His fingers scampered over the keys in a simple pattern that faintly soared. Despite the ringing in my ears, I recognized a sort of combination between the thumping theme from *The Killers* and the race music from *Ben-Hur*.

I let him go on for a bit, even though my head ached like hell. Suzi stood there smiling, taking in the rhapsody that hurt my ear. Finally, I reached out and interrupted, which was a bad thing, since it set him off wandering the room with his hands behind his back. His stare reminded me of Peter Lorre. His stature and size were similar to the actor's, but with a softness and sensitivity around the mouth that put me at ease.

I clasped him by the shoulders. "I want you to understand that Cromwell is completely blocked. Things are fine with Sturges now. He wants you back on the score for his western. And I'm pretty sure MGM won't have a problem with it anymore."

He dropped down onto a pastel green and yellow davenport and folded one hand over the other in his lap. "It is you who does not understand at all."

I looked at Suzi and then back at the composer, who had jumped back up. "The head of production and other top studio executives at MGM are threatening *me* now over my exclusive contract."

For a little guy, he could poke you in the chest with a stiff finger hard enough to make you sit down. "You may have fixed things up with Sturges' problems, but I have the problems now."

"I'm not sure I heard you correctly."

His mouth moved slowly. "Attorney problems."

So.

Even if I'd gotten Cromwell to end the trumped-up charge against

Sturges, the studio was taking a new tactic of threatening Rozsa.

The composer reached out to touch my upper arm, as if to steady himself, or to lend me a bit of his inspiration. "Besides, I don't like the score for this magnificent seven, so much. You heard it when you came in just now. It's all so lumpy-jumpy horsey-back riding." A vein swelled in his neck. His hands went up. "I've lost my muse. He can have it." Rozsa poked at my chest again. "Give it to Benny Hermann or Raskin or someone. I don't want my name on it."

I didn't understand a lot of that until later, but I saw Suzi poke her own finger at the little man and form one word with her firm lips: "Jerk."

* * * *

Weeks later, for reasons I may or may not have been a part of, MGM backed off its direct attempt to put UA out of business. They also backed off pressuring Sturges, for reasons I was sure I'd been a part of. I figured Cromwell was on a short leash, probably hiding out somewhere, waiting for our next go around. *Bring it on, fella.*

After finishing location shooting in Mexico, Sturges and his whole crew were back in town and had set up filming interior scenes at the Goldwyn Studios on Santa Monica Boulevard.

Norm wanted to go to the West Hollywood location, so he could meet Yul Brynner. I couldn't have cared less. I was just happy to see Steve McQueen again, who introduced me to his friend and fellow actor, James Coburn. The five of us, without Yul, ate dinner across the street at the Formosa Café. Sinatra sat at a dark table near the back with a very cute brunette. He raised his chin in greeting when he saw me and mouthed the single, friendly word, "Pally." I wiggled two fingers and having waved, moved on.

Sturges briefly took me aside and tried to thank me for getting him out of the murder frame. He ended up by giving me his pass to the studio and indicating that I could use it anytime. I ended up giving it to Norm, who kissed it.

Several courses of Chinese cuisine and rounds of drinks later, the director led us back to the UA screening room where we watched rushes from earlier that week. The scenes on the screen were a jumble, apparently making profound sense to the rest of the crowd.

Charles Bronson caught up with the gang around midnight and brought along Elmer Bernstein. The musician played a tune on a battered piano old enough to have accompanied Chaplin and Fairbanks during the silent era. "That, gentlemen, is the main theme from the film," Bernstein informed us.

No one in the room had heard it before, except me. They all gave a rousing cheer to the galloping Copland swing of the piece and passed around a bottle of Four Roses. Sturges immediately claimed that the sweeping theme would surely win an Oscar.

Maybe because of my weakened auditor nerve, I had the eerie feeling that I'd heard the tune once before… when Rozsa had played it at the Bel-Air. I kept the original composer's confidence and said nothing to the gang that night. And damned if the score didn't win at the next Academy Award ceremony ten months later. Which is about how long it took me to stop that lonely, weedy crime scene at the high school from haunting my dreams.

Still, every so often, I get brief flashes in my mind of those grainy newspaper photos of Jean Ellory's cold body lying there in the brush and the expressionless look in the eyes of her son, Jimmy.

DOUBLE INJEOPARDY

"Stop laughing. It isn't funny."

"Sure it is." I lean back in my creaking office chair and toss a green paperclip at Norman's head, which he deftly catches as it bounces off the left temple of his tortoise-shell glasses. *Impressive.*

"How was I supposed to know she was Debbie's stand in, Boss?" He's rueful. "She's a dead ringer."

Is he putting me on again? I hold up the latest copy of "The Hollywood Reporter." "If you read the trades like I do, you know the real Debbie Reynolds couldn't appear at the cheesy opening dedication of that Walk of Fame thing on Hollywood Boulevard."

He studies the magazine cover while I toy with another paperclip. "What the heck is Pat Boone doing in a Jules Verne movie?"

I tap the article further down the page about Debbie. "She's been back East since late January, shooting scenes for 'The Rat Race' with Tony Curtis."

He shrugs. "Well, at least I got to talk with Barbara Stanwyck. She looks pretty good, but not as fetching as when she was in 'Double Indemnity.'"

"Few of us are."

"She said to tell you thanks again, Mr. Wade, for your help with that kidnapping case."

Thinking back, I recall her husband never did pay my last bill. *Have to follow up on that.*

"So what am I going to do?" He waves a sealed #10 envelope. "I still have to serve Debbie with this summons and she hasn't stopped moving since she divorced Eddie. When's she due back in L.A?"

It is my turn to shrug. "I just saw her last week in that 'Gazebo' movie with Glen Ford."

"You know what they say…. 'She's so cute. She's almost perfect.'"

"If I didn't know better, Norm, I'd think you're in love."

"That's as silly as flying saucers."

Norman "Weirdo" Weirick talks like that all the time. He aspires to be a private investigator and has helped me in a couple of cases. He's shown reasonable potential, so I asked an attorney firm to give him a few processes to serve, as a test of his ability to track down people. Seemed harmless. Gave him experience in finding folks and ducking when they got mad for having been found.

"How many more of these papers do I have to hand out, Mr. Wade?"

I decide to go easy on him. He's not a kid any longer and his heart is in the right place. "Let's call it a day and grab some lunch."

He brightens. "I'll drink to that. Orange cream soda!"

Ugh! He seems sincere, but probably still putting me on.

* * * *

We exit my office at the back of the Brown Derby and walk through the main restaurant. I salute Sandra Dee who is lunching with Bobby Darin. Norm and I enter the sandwich shop to the left of the entrance in time to see the TV over the counter broadcasting a news report about Jack Paar quitting "The Tonight Show," followed by a bulletin that a woman who looks like Debbie Reynolds has been run down and killed on Highland Avenue near the Paramount Theater.

"Good." Norm nods, sliding into a booth by the window and adjusting the location of the catsup bottle. "I like that Johnny Carson guy better."

My interest is on the dead woman. "Norm, did you happen to notice if anyone followed you when you were locating and serving that summons?"

"What? No." He adjusts his glasses and inspects the laminated menu. "At least I don't think so."

He may have led someone to the fake Debbie.

Norm rambles: "Did you happen to notice Superman is dating a mermaid in the Sunday comics?"

Someone who was after the real Debbie.

"A bunch of science fiction fans are getting together to discuss Heinlein's 'Starship Trooper' and they want me to put on a short lecture about the Captain Marvel vs. Superman lawsuit."

If so, I had put her and maybe him in jeopardy when I got him the process serving job.

"Captain Marvel was the Big Red Cheese and he had a talking tiger."

I'd better look into it.

"I think the tiger was named Tony or something. Hey, where are you going, Mr. Wade?"

* * * *

Back in my office, I call a real-world captain. Sometimes friend, Steve Seidman of the LAPD, says the dead woman was known as Kandy King, but her real name was Janice Gloover. There was a single witness to the hit-and-run, and no he can't tell me anything more, why?

I ring off and become even more suspicious the killer may have followed Norm from the attorneys when he tried to serve that summons. I should check in with the law office to find out who is involved with the legal case, but I hate dealing with low-life lawyers and can't be in two places at once. What I really want to do is to track down Kandy King's agent and see how she got the stand-in job. *Maybe Suzi can follow-up with the attorney firm.* I call my fiancé at Sunset Investigations.

Miss King's representation is listed in my wilted SAG directory as Ultra Talent in the Bradbury Building on Broadway next to the Grand Central Market. As it's a mild February day and still early in the afternoon, I take a chance and drive downtown, listening to the soothing theme from "A Summer Place" on the AM radio. I park my T-bird in the lot beside the Million Dollar Theatre where the marquee declares they are showing Boetticher's Legs Diamond movie.

Inside the open-air Bradbury, I ride the elevator cage to the fourth floor. I love the golden sunlight that streams down from the atrium to grant natural lighting to all the iron grillwork railing and banisters. The russet brick walls and diamond-patterned tile floors look exactly as they had in "D.O.A." and "I, The Jury," except for the fact those dark crime movies had been in shot in black-and-white.

I let my right palm slide lightly along the railing. I had almost taken a header over this same rail a couple of years ago while tracking down a stolen painting for Vincent Price. I grit my teeth and listen to the echoing clacks of my footsteps as I approach Ultra Talent's suite. I don't bother to knock, since the door is held partly open by a small iron statue of a Chinese dragon and I can hear voices muffled inside. The agency owner, R. C. Higgins, is standing close to Natalie Wood. She's dressed in a tennis sweater and skirt, with her hair in a cute pixie cut. He's dressed in a gray two-piece with a ruffled and askew tie. She eases onto the arm of an overstuffed couch positioned in the center of a Navajo rug.

He stands erect, next to a small wet-bar in front of a hideous Mondrian-designed wallpaper, and gestures with a Jack Daniel's bottle.

"So, Nat…" He clears his throat. "I'm telling you, that Young Savages movie will be a turkey." He pours bourbon into a glass and hands it to her.

She sets it down without drinking or looking my way. "But Bobby and I have such great chemistry together. That's part of the reason I married him."

"Not on screen, you don't." The agent slicks back his raven hair. Dark eyebrows over a piercing stare capture me. He sees me stepping in from the doorway. "Can I help you?" The question is a dry as a crouton.

I fish out one of my business cards and hand it to him.

He smirks. "Stan Wade. Nice stage name."

I let the comment go. "Did you send Kandy King to impersonate Debbie Reynolds at the Walk of Fame ceremony?"

His eyes move from me to his client on the edge of the sofa. "Yeah, she's good at that, but otherwise a real pain in the ass. So what?"

"I guess you haven't heard. She's dead."

Natalie bounds up. There's a large gift box next to her on the end table beside a French phone.

I study the agent's face. *Stony reaction.* "She was hit by a car in West Hollywood."

Higgins takes a step back and steadies himself against the bar. "Jesus."

Natalie puts on a large pair of sunglasses and picks up the gift box with a chinchilla wrap half hanging out. "I should be running along now, Randy." She heads briskly for the exit.

It dawns on me I've interrupted an early afternoon liaison. I call after her: "Loved you in 'Rebel With a Cause.'"

"Out." Her voice echoes from the hallway. "Without a Cause."

"Yeah," Higgins grunts. "She was great in that western with John Wayne, too. She'll survive, with a little solid representation." He takes a long, slow drink and then stares at me. "What the hell am I talking about? Janice is dead? Are you serious, man?"

"It was on the news." I relate what details I know and ask if he has any idea who may have had it in for her.

He spreads his arms wide. "She was a sweetheart. Everybody loved her. Why are you shaking your head?"

"I thought you said she was a pain in the ass."

"That was before, okay? Now, she's a doll and wonderful talent with a bright fut—" He sits down hard on the couch.

Seems genuinely shocked. "Did she have any close friends or associates?"

"Yeah...."

"And? Like who?"

"She rooms, uh, roomed with a friend, Dori Williams. I can get you the address."

"Thanks. She have a boyfriend?"

"Dead... Wow!" Randy Higgins seems genuinely stunned. "We could all go at anytime."

"Yeah, none of us are getting out of this alive." I take the empty glass from his hand. "Boyfriend?"

"Oh, yeah. I don't recall the guy's name, but he sure could drink gin and tonics. I paid for six of them during dinner one time."

"He have a name?"

"Uh, Eddie or Freddie, I think."

Great. "What'd he look like?"

"Uh, big, blond, dark tan. Maybe a Muscle Beach guy. Sorry, that's all I got."

"No sweat. What's that address?"

He goes over to a corner desk and scribbles on a note pad. I see it's the Wilshire Boulevard apartments. "Thanks again."

The agent pours another drink. "Sure, sure." Since he doesn't offer me one, I leave him alone with his Kentucky booze and stunned grief.

* * * *

It's coming onto rush hour, and there's a good chance Dori Williams will be getting home soon, so I grab the Hollywood Freeway and find the address of her apartment building, which I'd forgotten is more famously known as The Bryson. It's a white, triple stacked affair, ten stories tall in a Beaux Arts style. Chandler mentioned the place once in one of his novels and again when he co-wrote the screenplay for "Double Indemnity."

I park my Ford at the curb on a side street and walk to the corner of Rampart and Wilshire. While waiting for the light to change so I can cross the busy boulevard, I see a Caddy pause and turn, driven by a young girl. In the back seat, an old guy in a conservative suit sits next to a wooden dummy in top hat and tux. The old guy stares straight ahead, but the dummy is wearing a monocle and looks right at me. *Only in L.A.*

Once out of the bright February sunshine and into the cool interior of marble floors and masonry stairs, I pause to check the mailbox listings and find the apartment where Kandy King, born Janice Gloover, is supposed to have lived and buzz the buzzer at 202. The door opens as far as the chain lock allows and I see a female eye with too much makeup.

"Who are you and what do you want?"

I smile, hold up a business card, and ask to speak with Dori Williams. Nicely manicured fingers take the card and close the door. I wait and then she calls out, "If this is about Janice, I already talked to the cops."

"I know," I lie. "But I have a few more questions. It's about Debbie Reynolds."

There's a beat of silence and then: "Oh, what the hell." She throws back the lock and I'm welcomed in by a fiercely yapping miniature schnauzer. She's holding the dog in her arm as it growls like a buzz-saw and slobbers on the sleeve of her light blue blouse.

"Quiet, Bitsy."

I smell the scent of Johnson's floor wax and notice a small vase of cut flowers, slightly wilted.

Bitsy whines, cocks its head, and gives me a soulful look from under fluffy-white bangs.

I watch the young woman bend and place the licking fuzz-ball on a tattered cushion next a TV stereo consol cluttered with framed photos. There's a trimness to her outfit, her pearl earrings tucked under medium-length brunette hair, and the plain blue pill-box hat at the back of her head. I get the impression she's dressed up to look like Jackie, the wife of the Massachusetts Senator who just announced running for President. "Nice outfit."

She straightens her skirt. "I was at the funeral home making arrangements. Thought something sort of formal would be nice." No tears.

I continue to smile. "How are you coping?"

She sighs, indicating I can sit in a kitchen chair over beside a TV tray still covered with the remains of last night's chicken dinner. "Well enough." She eases into a winged chair which doesn't match any other furniture in the room. "Would you like some coffee?"

"No. I'm good."

"Good. What do you want to know?"

"As Janice's roommate, what can you tell me about her?"

Bitsy's tiny chin rests on crossed paws atop a Flubbadub chew toy. The tips of twin pink tongues peek out.

Dori plucks at her sleeve. She looks down, concentrating. "She taught me everything I know about acting in this town, but now I've got a job as a typist and script-girl at M-G-M."

"Good for you. So tell me more about Janice and her work as Kandy King."

"Well, she came from Cincinnati two years ago. Doesn't have any family there or here. And not much chance of ever making the big time at the studios. Her career just wasn't going anywhere, except for stand-in jobs."

"Oh?"

"She— she had too many outside interests. Her heart wasn't in it all the time. Just for kicks."

Good kicks or bad kicks? "What other interests? Men?"

"Men and surfing. That's how we met. Out at Seal Beach last summer. I'm going out later today, if you care to join us."

A window air-conditioner kicks on behind her. Bitsy barks once and lies back down.

I think of Suzi. "Tell me a bit more about your roommate."

Dori begins to unpin her hat. "She ran around with a guy who drank a lot and surfed, but the guy was a little creepy about religion. Sort of a Beat who planned to join a communist commune or something."

Interesting.

She picks up a pack of Kent cigarettes and rotates it in her hands while talking. "He liked doing it with Janice when she'd dress up as a certain movie star. She was damn lucky to be able to impersonate film stars like Marilyn, Lana and Debbie."

"This guy have a name?"

"We called him Mickey the Mouth behind his back. I'm not sure what his full name is." She gets up and holds the back of her left wrist against her forehead. "Look, if you don't mind, I'm totally drained and need some sleep. You might find Mickey down at the beach, if it's not too late."

"I understand, fully. Thanks for your time." I make to leave and am tempted to ask one more thing… but the weariness in her eyes changes my mind. "I might check back later, if you don't mind."

Bitsy jumps up and runs around in circles, barking as if auditioning for a part as Lassie's mini-companion.

I pat the critter's tiny noggin and smile once more. We part ways as close pals.

* * * *

I consider canvassing the neighborhood, but am beginning to get heart-attack serious about the jeopardy Debbie Reynolds could be in, if my hunch is right. So, I swing by the office and call my gal Suzi who says the summons from the attorneys was simply a minor court appearance related to her divorce from Eddie Fisher. "Not much there, Standy. Want me to keep digging?"

"No, honey. But I think I should warn her. Did you get her number?"

"Actually, I have it here in my notes. Hold on." I grab a well-chewed pencil as I hear paper rattling on the other end of the line. *Sounds like a blazing fire.* "Here it is."

I jot the number down on the back of a flyer sent to me from an insurance company about a stolen statue from a gallery back East. Then, I tell Suzi I love her, and place a call to the Debbie's residence. Her maid answers and says Miss Reynolds is not in at the moment. I can only leave my name, number, and word she might be in danger.

I check my watch. *Getting late, but if I make it down to Seal Beach, I might find that surfer dude.*

* * * *

I stop for a fill-up at an Eagle gas station and drive south on the 405 to the Coast Highway. At Seal Beach off 9th Street, I pass a trailer park, a motel, and a cantina. Parking between two station-wagons, I stare out at the gray, incoming swells of the Pacific Ocean and hear their wet rumbling thunder. I had tried riding the waves in the early 1950s while attending USC, but it hadn't taken. *Left it all behind me.*

I take off my shoes and socks, roll up my pants legs, and shuffle through the sand. There are two beach fires for keeping warm and roasting hot dogs. There's a harsh smell of burning driftwood and a touch of cooked seaweed.

Three different guys beating bongo drums under a stripped beach umbrella. The place sounds like the inside of a Jiffy Pop popcorn container about to explode. A cute couple plays tonsil tennis.

There's Dori. She's wearing a beavertail wet suit with the flap which wraps around under her crotch and leaves her legs uncovered. *Cowabonga! Stay out of the tumbler.*

A big guy with shoulders no wider than a Buick rose up before us. "I'm Sailor. What's your beef?"

Sailor Whatsyourbeef wore a large jaw, wet hair and short, ill-fitting vest.

"Easy, boy." Dori presses a tiny palm on his hairless chest. "It's okay. Be nice. Say hello to a friend."

"Friend." He nods like a stallion and trots off.

She looks up at me. "So you decided to come out after all."

"That guy's a giant."

"Sailor had the hots for Kandy, but her boyfriend slugged him."

"You're telling me somebody beat that big guy up?"

"I told you Mickey is a tough customer."

The kissing couple approach us. He wears a tattered blue t-shirt and a church key on a chain around his neck. His hair is long, blond and bleached. The girl has her hair tied back in a pony tail, smiles with green eyes and wears a purple bathrobe. "This is Moonpuppy and Catgirl."

The girl kneels in the sand and opens an Igloo cooler full of Cokes and Coors and sandwiches. When the guy hands me a bag of potato chips, I can't help noticing the surfer knots on the tops of his feet and knees from a lifetime of paddling to catch up with a wall of glass.

"You wanna try it?" Dori pushes a board into my hands. "I've got a pair of Katin trunks in the back of the VW van. You can change there and shower after at the lifeguard station."

I gaze out at the waves of nostalgia. *What the hell. Why not?*

* * * *

Her stick is a nine-foot-long board and called a logger with no fins and a square tail. Mine is a cigar-box surfboard know as a Catalina Hollow. I had one like it once.

She looks at her surf watch, timing the sound of the breakers. "Surf's up!"

And then we're trotting toward the meager three-foot surf, hoping to catch a pipe ride. It all comes back to me in a rush; the getting vertical on my log, the riding it until the curl collapses.

In the water, everyone lays flat and begins to paddle out. Once beyond the surf line, we sit up. The waves lift us slowly up and down as the rhythm of the tide begins to roll in with growing strength. I see a beautiful five-foot wave coming toward us. It forms into a perfect crescent shape; a rhino. The swell moves toward us, a green gift from the center of the sea. We prone out on our boards and start paddling.

I hurry to catch the swell. The wave passes under us and lifts us high above the beach. Then… then we stand and shout at the curl. Halfway down the face of the party wave, I feel her drop into the pocket beside me. I crouch down low, shuffle up on the nose of the board like Quasimodo, and ride the heavy cigar box, shooting out of the green room and into the chop. I glide and crawl back to shore, exhilarated.

Maybe surfing took with me after all. Maybe I had been the one to leave it behind like the wave not taken. *And maybe, at age thirty, it's still not too late.*

* * * *

This whole case seems to be going nowhere at the speed of light. I call it a night and go grab a Chef Boy-ar-dee spaghetti dinner with Suzi at her apartment. She's great in the kitchen. And everywhere else. Tonight she greets me with a new hair style: Thick blonde cut short at the shoulders, plus wide-set eyes and supple lips. She says she had lunch with her close friend, Lauren Bacall.

Name dropper. I hold her in my arms and unzip her short, sheath-cut dress made of pink and white straw lace. We watch "Lawman" and "Maverick" on television and go to bed for a little pillow talk.

Later, I confess about my current case. "I'm not sure what to do."

Suzi snuggles nest to me from behind. "If you think she's in danger…. If you think she was the real target, Standy, you have to warn her."

"I did. But it feels like I've already done too much. It's none of my business."

"Yes, it is. You know it is and you feel you haven't done enough. That's all. So…."

"So, I should go and keep an eye on things. Maybe that'll protect her."

"Good."

"Yeah, you're right. It is my business."

And sleep slowly rolls in like silent surf.

* * * *

In my dream, a black-and-white clown pretends to be Oswald the Lucky Rabbit in Cincinnati. He's sings a chorus of, "All I do the whole night through is dream of you."

Suzi nudges my lower back and says I'm snoring.

I wake in the morning, shower, shave with the Norelco Suzi

bought me for Christmas, and scoot over to Debbie Reynolds house to again warn her of what feels like an increasing threat. *Maybe I can offer my protective services.*

It's a massive mansion on Greenway Drive in Beverly Hills overlooking the seventh hole of the LA Country Club. Her maid answers the door when I ring the bell; a little bitty biddy who ushers me in to meet her husband, the chauffeur. Both are in their sixties and tell me Miss Reynolds is outside checking the locks on all the windows and entrances with her new bodyguard and a private investigator named Stan Wade.

"Stan Wade?"

"Here's his card."

It was mine all right.

Debbie walks into the living room from the back of the house, past ornately-framed Italian landscapes and upholstered French furniture. She's stunning in a wide-brimmed hat and a yellow and orange swim suit. There's a beefy guy with her who must be the new bodyguard and a lean character in thin tie, holding an unlit pipe. The skinny guy's voice sounds oddly familiar. It is much like my own, only higher pitched. *Norman is doing me.*

"Oh, there you are, Weirick." He points the stem of his pipe at me. "Miss Reynolds, this is my assistant, Norman Weirick."

The maid quietly addresses her mistress. "He claimed to be another private detective. Gave his name as Sam Spade, or something."

The bodyguard gives me a fishy look from under his tight brows and butch haircut. He's dressed like a jungle guide in a Tarzan movie. Light brown shorts with a wide leather belt. Gray shirt with flapped pockets and thick sleeves rolled over big biceps. A dab of white zinc on the bridge of his nose.

Debbie raises her chin. "Jack, I think you should escort this man from my house."

"Now wait. I'll go, but...."

"Damn right, you'll go."

I glance daggers at Norm who rocks back on his heels. "Easy with him, Jack, my man. I might need his help... later."

The bodyguard grabs my upper right arm and I smell the distinctive odor of Sen-Sen breath freshener. I look down at his knobby knees. "Maybe I could just hang ten here, huh?"

"You can hang ten outside, hot-dogger."

I take a shot in the dark. "You're name's not Jack. It's Mickey." That freezes him, but I can see the fire inside bringing him to a quick boil. *Hell, might as well fan the flames.* "You're the guy who ran down Miss Reynolds's stand-in." That stops him. I study his eyes. There's not much there, except the first hint of panic. "You're her surfer boyfriend. You like kinky sex with fake movie stars." Fire seemed to light the back of his pupils. "And now you're stalking the real Debbie Reynolds."

"Okay, asswipe."

I should have figured a guy dressed as a jungle explorer would carry a knife. His hand goes to the pocket of his safari shorts. I hear a snick. A sharply-pointed four-inch blade flicks out of the black handle.

I don't usually pack heat, since Suzi can shoot the pips off the six of spades. Nonetheless, my first instinct is to go for him, but the voice of experience tells me to grab a cushion or something to absorb his thrust.

The corners of his mouth tweak at my hesitation. He whirls around, his face contorted in mad dominance, the veins and tendons in his neck as thick as nightcrawlers.

A little dark-haired girl of about four toddles into the room. "Momma?" Debbie calls out. "Get back, Carrie."

At first I think he's going to go for the chauffeur, but he pushes the old guy aside and reaches for Debbie.

I dash forward. The maid grabs the child's ceramic doll and slams her mistresses' attacker in the back of the head, one, two, three.

The beefy guy growls through yellow teeth. He's pumped with adrenaline. Norman drops his pipe, steps in deftly, and cold-cocks Jungle Jerk with a solid uppercut I couldn't have done better myself. Mickey spins around once and takes out a floor lamp as he goes down hard and lays stiff on his face.

I catch the fumbled knife. *Wipe out!*

Debbie plants a long kiss on Norm's half-opened mouth.

* * * *

The police are called and arrive to take the body guard away on assault charges.

Later, the eye witness identifies Mickey as the guy who drove the car that ran down Debbie's look-alike. Dori and the surfers identify him as Janice's boozing boyfriend.

Suzi, was right. It was my business, after all.

* * * *

Norman comes by the office the next day to explain and apologize. "I love her, Mr. Wade. She's so cute!"

"It's Debbie, you're talking about, right?" I'm still pissed at being impersonated. "You could have been in deep jeopardy. But everybody loves her, Norm. That's why I thought maybe the killer might, too. I called ahead and tried to warn her."

"I know." He nods. "That's why she hired the bodyguard."

Wait! "Do you mean she hired that guy because of my phone call?"

"I think that's what he wanted all along." He nods ruefully again. "That's part of the reason he killed the other girl. To spook Debbie into wanting protection. Then he just showed up."

This realization is stunning. By trying to warn her, I'd panicked her into a rash decision and danger. The jeopardy she'd been in was partly my own doing. "So I'm the one who put her in…."

"Yep. Looks that way, Mr. Wade. But how'd you know he was the killer?"

Now, I'm the one who feels a little stampeded. Maybe I'd done too much after all.

"Mr. Wade?" Norm waves. "Boss?"

"What?"

"Indeed, what. What was it tipped you off?"

"Oh." I hear myself swallow. "Sin-sin."

"Come again?"

"I saw his surfer knob knees and smelled his heavy breath fresher. The killer was known to be a heavy drinker of gin. And you know the old saying?"

"The one about the wages of gin is breath? I get it." He pushes his specks up his nose. "You are one super detective, Boss."

Sure. I shake off the feeling of being an unwilling accomplice. "And the next time you disguise yourself as me, loose the pipe, Norm. You know, I quit smoking last year."

"What? And give up show biz? Great Krypton!"

He's putting me on again. I throw the twin of the green paperclip at his noggin.

The weirdo catches that one, too. In his teeth.

A PRIVATE EYE'S WORST DAY

There's a bright golden haze on the Hollywood sign and the smog is as high as a sea gull's right eye, as the wind comes right behind the rain. I open the mail and wince at the reminder of how much I owe. *Five kinds of bills and no way to pay them.*

I call around Los Angeles and Anaheim to reach a few of my past clients, like Uncle Walt or John Ford, hoping to stumble into even a small investigation. Everybody is fine. They have no problems. And Suzi's out of town on that Kennedy case. I'm the only one, it seems, who needs something to do. The most exciting thing to happen lately was watching "Oklahoma" on NBC's Saturday Night at the Movies.

I call a couple of other agencies, even as far as Palmdale, thinking I might pick up a little work from them. They can't think of a thing to throw my way right now, but they'll get back to me if anything turns up. "I know I owe you big time, Stan, but things are tight now because of the beefed-up security with all the X-15 and astronaut activity around Edwards Air Force Base. Maybe in a couple of months."

Yeah, and maybe the sun will come up in the west.

I begin to regret getting into the P.I. biz. It had been a wonderful profession when I'd started here in a tiny office in the old Faraday Building, but when that burned down, all I could get was bouncer duty and an office in the back of the Brown Derby. Lately, the bottom seems to have fallen out of the market and things are as tight as Jack Benny's fist on a buffalo nickel. People are solving their own crimes or cops have become smarter and more proficient than in past years when I apprenticed with Mr. P. in the early '50s.

What am I going to do?

Typically, someone would always come through the office door and offer me cash to investigate their boss, or wife, or son, or partner. Right now, I'd be ecstatic with a lost dog or stolen boat case. It would put money in my bank account and give me an excuse to get some fresh sea air.

The phone sits there, dormant as a paper weight. Maybe it's even put on a few pounds.

Wait a minute! I don't need a case to go out into the fresh air. I can take a stroll or hike just for the hell of it. And if I walk in the right direction, say, down toward the ocean side, or over to the racetrack, I might stumble into a small paying job. *Why didn't I think of that earlier?*

I stuff a couple of business cards into my wallet, in case I run into a good prospect and lock the office behind me. Passing through the main restaurant area of the Brown Derby, I catch sight of a bunch of photographers snapping shots of Doris Day and Rock Hudson together in a booth under sketches of Groucho and Garbo. *Must be making another "Pillow Talk" flick. Too bad I don't have them as a client.*

Stepping into the warm wind blowing in from the coast, my heart begins to race, as I glance across the street at the Ambassador Hotel. Maybe I'll witness a robbery or a highjacking. Maybe I'll stumble into an old girlfriend who's had her jewelry stolen. *Yeah, right.*

I stop at the intersection of Wilshire and Vermont and watch a bus moan past. I look at the passenger's faces, but nobody seems distressed; nobody signals for help. The light changes and I cross the street without bumping into an old friend down on his luck or a mysterious dame being followed.

I weave my way through a small crowd of expressionless souls coming in and going out of an Owl Drugs next to a travel agency. I stand in front of the window and stare at the posters for Paris and Hawaii. It would be sweet if I somehow snagged an assignment that would take me back to those places again. Diamond smuggles or hitmen. Exotic locals with colorful names like Versailles and Honolulu.

There's a bum seated beneath the window. He's been watching, but I haven't said a word. He holds out a claw of a hand, palm up, and I find a few coins in my pocket to give him. He thanks me, but doesn't mention any secret password or warning. *Crap.*

I like the hidden history and aviation intrigue of the area. Edwards Air Base had been the site of several of my best investigations. Last year's payroll robbery had been my biggest and most lucrative. Unfortunately, security is much tighter now, so I've had to rely entirely on the private sector to keep the Stan Wade, LA PI agency alive.

I watch a sooty gull making lazy circles in the sky. My stomach rumbles and I consider buying a 5th Avenue candy bar from the drug store. Instead, I become more determined than ever. There *must* be some sort of work around this damned city for a skilled and efficient P.I.

Maybe if I put a tail on some random sidewalk pedestrian. It would at least be good practice and maybe I'll luck into something.

I pick a likely prospect. Tall guy, blue suit, red tie, about forty, glasses and trimmed mustache. He's crossing 6th Street near La Fayette Park. I shove my hands into my front trouser pockets and amble along behind him, keeping a couple of other folks between us. He has no idea I'm following him.

We pass a peanut stand and two taxi cabs parked outside a Hilton hotel and turn the corner, which is actually more of an oval. One of my old girlfriends used to live nearby. The one who had her diamond necklace stolen while she was auditioning for a part in a musical at Warner Brothers. *Wonder why they never wrote a romantic musical about La La Land.*

There are fewer people walking here in this quiet neighborhood, so I have to fall back even further in order not to be noticed by my quarry. For some reason, my palms are sweating. Usually this is a sign that I'm on edge or embarrassed. I flex my fingers, trying to shake off the feeling I'm the one being followed.

I know there's a department store a block further up the street and another bank beyond that. Tall Guy is probably headed for the bank. Maybe he's a courier carrying thousands of dollars in his blue suit.

I decide not to follow him into the bank. Instead, I find another guy, younger, fatter, and coming out the entrance and I pick up his trail. We walk briskly along, until he goes into the front of the old Hilton hotel. I go inside this time and wait in the lobby while he makes a phone call and uses the Men's room.

When he comes out, I pick up after him again. We turn left, then right. I stay with him past the bus stop. We're moving along nicely in the warm morning sunshine which slices down between the buildings. After we hot-foot it across the crowed street—and just as I'm getting tired of this silly game—Young guy walks up and greets Tall Guy!

I immediately hang back. I turn around to face the other direction, embarrassed. How childish of me. I'm going to have to buy a newspaper from the vending machine here next to the fire hydrant. Yeah and that way, I can search the Want Ads for a decent job.

I realize I've given my last coins to the bum outside the travel agency. There's a slot in the vending machine that takes dollar bills. I reach into my back pocket for my wallet and discover that it's gone. I know I had it with me when I left the office.

I look around at all the people coming and going up and down the street.

I'm excited. Elated, even! Oh, what a beautiful morning. Finally, I have a case!

Everything's going my way.

ABOUT THE AUTHOR

Award-winning author, John Hegenberger has produced more than a dozen books since mid-2015, including several popular series: Stan Wade LAPI in 1959, Eliot Cross Columbus-based PI in 1988, and Tripleye, the first PI agency on Mars. His latest novel, The Pandora Block, is a high-tech, international thriller. Several of his short stories have appeared in Black Cat Mystery Magazine. His Stan Wade, LA PI novel, SPYFALL, won a 2016 award at Killer Nashville. Discover more at www.johnhegenberger.com

www.ingramcontent.com/pod-product-compliance
Lightning Source LLC
Chambersburg PA
CBHW020649130626
46552CB00003B/1460